MW01602386

PALESTINE
Coloring Book For Kids
With Interesting Facts

GRANT
PUBLISHING

This Book Belongs To

_____

INTRODUCTION

Welcome to the "Palestine Coloring Book for Kids" – part of our exciting coloring book series! Get ready for a colorful adventure where you'll learn all about this incredible Asian nation, Palestine.

With each stroke of your crayon, you'll uncover fascinating facts about Palestine's history, culture, and landmarks. From its beautiful landscapes to rich cultural traditions, this coloring book is your ticket to exploring the beauty and diversity of Palestine.

Grab your favorite colors, and let's start coloring our way into discovering Palestine! 🖌🎨

TIPS

This coloring book is your passport to exploring the world through colors and creativity. Here are some tips to make your coloring journey even more enjoyable:

Take Breaks: Coloring is lots of fun, but remember to take short breaks if your hand gets tired.

Color Inside the Lines: Use your crayons or colored pencils to stay inside the lines.

Ask Questions: If you're curious about something you're coloring, don't hesitate to ask.

Hold Your Pencils: Hold your crayons or colored pencils gently, like you're holding a spoon. This way, you'll have better control and make beautiful pictures.

Remember, there's no rush in the world of coloring. Take your time, enjoy the process, and let your creativity soar! ✏️🖍️✨

CHECK OUT OUR BOOK SERIES

Ready for more adventures? Don't forget to check out the other books in our series! You can explore different countries and cultures through fun facts and coloring. Let's embark on a colorful journey around the world together! ●■✹

Check out our website for more books

www.grantpublishingltd.co.uk

CONTINENT

Palestine is located in the continent of Asia.

NAME

The official name of Palestine is the State of Palestine.

COUNTRY

Palestine is located in the Middle East, specifically in the eastern part of the Mediterranean region.

COUNTRY

Palestine is bordered by Israel to the east and north, Egypt to the southwest, Jordan to the east, and the Mediterranean Sea to the west.

CITIES

Some major cities in Palestine include Jerusalem, Bethlehem, Ramallah, and Gaza City.

SIZE

Palestine covers an area of approximately 6,220 square kilometers (2,400 square miles).

CAPITAL

The capital city of Palestine is Jerusalem, and its administrative center is Ramallah.

LANDMARKS

Palestine is home to several significant landmarks, including the Dome of the Rock, the Church of the Nativity, and the Western Wall.

PEOPLE

The estimated population of Palestine is around 5 million people.

PEOPLE

Palestinians are the people who primarily inhabit Palestine.

LANGUAGE

The official languages of Palestine are Arabic and Hebrew.

ANTHEM

The national anthem of Palestine is called "Biladi" ("My Country").

CURRENCY

The currency used in Palestine is the Israeli new shekel (ILS).

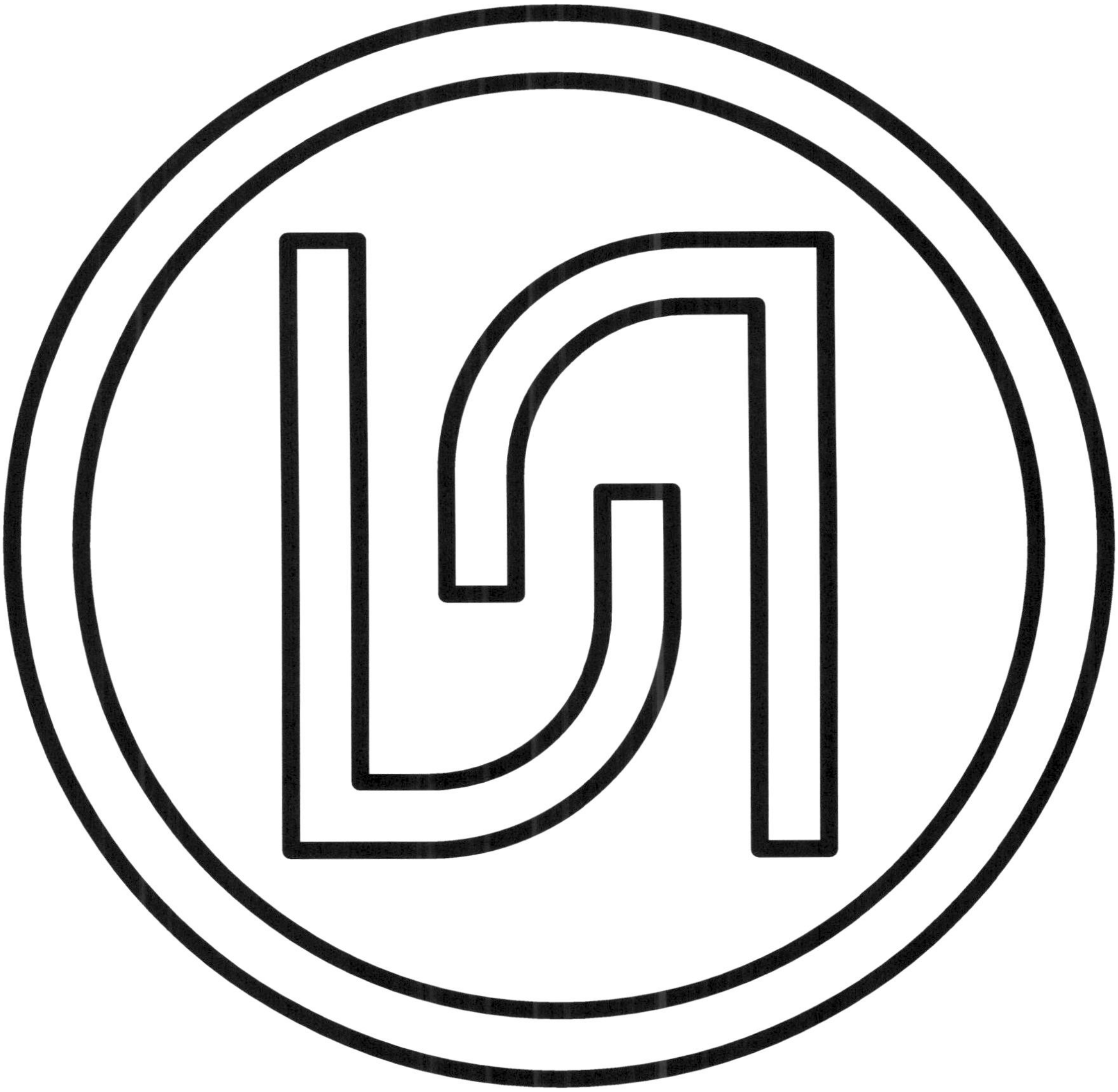

HISTORY

Palestine has a rich and complex history, with cultural and historical connections dating back thousands of years.

FLAG

The Palestinian flag consists of three horizontal stripes of black, white, and green colors, with a red triangle on the hoist side.

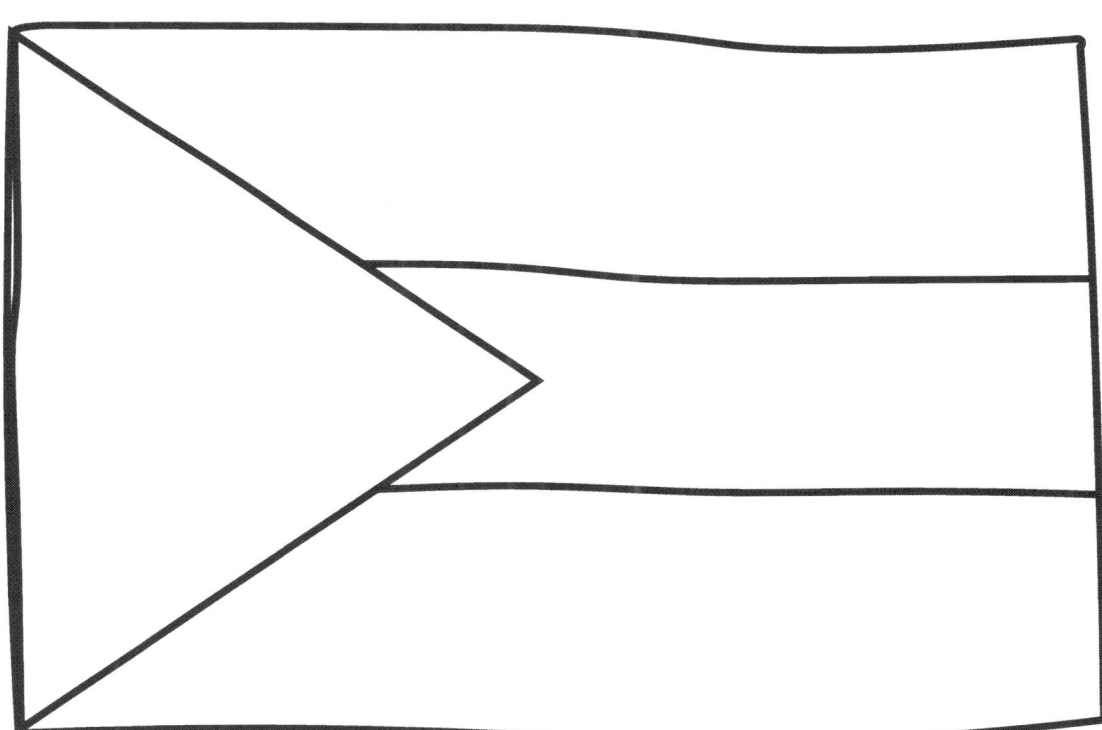

RELIGION

The majority of Palestinians practice Islam, while a minority practice Christianity.

DESERT

The Negev Desert and parts of the Judean Desert are located in Palestine.

CLIMATE

Palestine has a Mediterranean climate, characterized by hot, dry summers and mild, rainy winters.

MOUNTAIN

The highest peak in Palestine is Mount Hermon, located in the Golan Heights region.

RIVER

The Jordan River, one of the major rivers in the region, flows along the eastern border of Palestine.

FESTIVALS

Ramadan is an important month of fasting and spiritual reflection for Muslims in Palestine.

SYMBOL

The national animal of Palestine is the Arabian Oryx, which is an antelope species.

SYMBOL

The olive tree is an important symbol of Palestinian culture and heritage, representing peace, rootedness, and resilience.

ANIMALS

Palestine is home to a diverse range of wildlife, including ibex, hyenas, wolves, foxes, and various bird species.

SPORTS

Football (soccer) is a popular sport in Palestine, and the national team participates in international competitions.

DISHES

Palestinian cuisine is diverse and influenced by various Mediterranean and Middle Eastern flavors.

DISHES

Palestinian cuisine is rich in flavors and includes dishes like falafel, hummus, maqluba (a rice and vegetable dish), and knafeh (a sweet pastry).

CUSTOMS

The Arabic coffee cup, known as "finjan," is an important symbol of hospitality and is often used in Palestinian households.

GLOSSARY

- Country: A place where people live. Every country has its own special things like food, music, and more!

- Continent: A big piece of land with many countries on it. Our Earth has seven continents!

- River: A long, flowing stream of water that can be big or small.

- Ocean: The hugest water body in the world, full of water creatures and mysteries!

- Cuisine: Fancy word for food! Every country has its own special cuisine with yummy dishes.

- History: The stories from a long, long time ago. They tell us about what happened before we were born.

- Population: The number of people living in a country. Some countries have lots of people, and some have just a few.

GLOSSARY

- Ethnic Minority: Special groups of people with their own customs and traditions.

- Language: The words people use to talk to each other. Every country has its own language.

- Landscape: What a place looks like. Some places have tall mountains, while others have wide deserts.

- Climate: The type of weather in a country. It can be hot, cold, or just right!

- National Dish: A special food that a country is famous for and loves to eat.

- Flag: A country's special colors and symbols on a piece of cloth. Flags are like a country's signature!

ABOUT THE AUTHOR

Thank you for choosing our book. At Grant Publishing, we're passionate about creating educational and exciting books to spark your child's curiosity about the world. Our mission is to make learning a delightful adventure.

By exploring the pages of this coloring book, your child has embarked on a journey to discover the beauty of different countries and cultures. We encourage you to keep nurturing their love for learning and exploration.

If you enjoyed this book and found it both fun and educational, we'd love to hear from you! Please consider leaving a review on Amazon to share your thoughts and help other families discover the joy of learning through our books.

Stay curious, keep coloring, and let's continue exploring the world together!

With warmest regards,
Grant Publishing

THE END

Made in the USA
Las Vegas, NV
17 October 2024

97002881R00022